The Secret Dinosaur
Book 2
Hunters Attack!

N.S.Blackman

D0542238

All Rights Reserved
Published by Dinosaur Books Ltd, London
This edition: 2015
www.dinosaurbooks.co.uk
Dinoteks™ Sonya McGilchrist

ISBN 978-0-9927525-1-4
British Library Cataloguing in Publication Data
A CIP catalogue record for this book is available from
the British Library

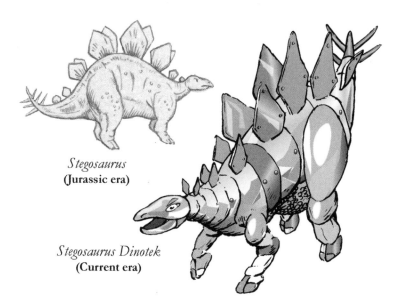

Stegosaurus
(Jurassic era)

Stegosaurus Dinotek
(Current era)

The Secret Dinosaur - 2

by N.S.Blackman

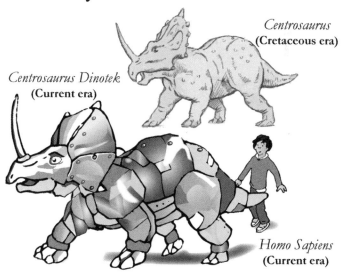

Centrosaurus
(Cretaceous era)

Centrosaurus Dinotek
(Current era)

Homo Sapiens
(Current era)

Also available in the **Dinoteks** series

The Secret Dinosaur Book 1
The Secret Dinosaur Book 3
The Secret Dinosaur Book 4
The Lost Dinosaur (for younger readers)

Visit www.dinoteks.com for the latest titles,
puzzles and activities featuring the Dinoteks!

The Dinoteks

Next time you go to a museum look out for the dusty old dinosaur that nobody else is interested in.

There's usually one.

Most people think it's just an old museum statue, left over from the days when models weren't very realistic.

But if you know what to look for, and if you are really lucky, you might discover an amazing secret.

Dinoteks are more than statues or models or even dinosaurs.

Dinoteks are living machines.

www.dinoteks.com

For
Emily, Bethany,
Ethan,
Ella and Liv

The Story So Far

....

How everyone forgot the Dinoteks

It was supposed to happen like this: the mechanical dinosaur was supposed to wait for visitors at the museum entrance.

"Welcome," he would say. "My name is Protos. Come with me and let's imagine that we are travelling back through time, back to the world of the dinosaurs…"

And then Protos was supposed to take the visitors into a room full of living machine dinosaurs – Dinoteks, every bit as fantastic as he was.

But it didn't happen.

Something went wrong.

The Professor who had created

the Dinoteks disappeared and in their room at the museum, one by one, the creatures fell asleep. Their batteries failed and they froze where they were, becoming just metal statues.

Protos was the last one left awake.

He looked out of the museum window expecting any moment to see the Professor hurrying up the steps clutching his bag full of papers and gadgets and special tools.

Protos watched and waited. And after a whole day he went to stand in his little room next to the Dinosaur Gallery.

"I'll just practise my speech," he said to himself. "Ahem! Ladies and gentlemen, girls and boys, imagine travelling back in time to the Jurassic era. Close your eyes and picture it. A hundred million years seems like a long time but really it's just the blink of an eye... really, just the blink of an..."

And with one last yawn his head nodded and Protos slept too.

******

Clunk!

Many years passed and gradually everybody forgot about the Dinoteks. Dust settled on them, burying them like fossils.

The door to their room was no longer opened and its hinges became stiff with rust.

New models arrived at the museum, made of plastic not metal. They weren't alive, but they looked much more realistic.

People stopped coming into the little room to look at Protos.

They thought he was rather funny – just an odd looking statue made out of scraps of metal.

Until one day Marlin Maxton arrived…

****

In *The Secret Dinosaur* Marlin brought Protos back to life and began an amazing adventure.

You can read the full story in Book 1.

Visit www.dinoteks.com to find out more.

BUT NOW…on to Book 2!

It's time for the next adventure to begin…

Chapter One

. . . .

The Silent Visitor

The creature was so big that its head easily reached up to the top floor of the house.

It arrived in the middle of the night, stepping over the garden fence, and nobody saw it.

The house had three windows upstairs and the creature seemed to know exactly which one it was looking for.

It leaned down and nudged the edge of the wooden frame. The window opened and the creature lifted something from its back and lowered it into the house.

A moment later it was gone, slipping into the mist like a ghost, as

silently and quickly as it had arrived.

There was no sign that it had ever been there, except in the grass underneath the window.

Pressed down very deep in the lawn was a massive, three-toed footprint.

****

Marlin Maxton woke up to find himself in bed the wrong way round.

His trainers were still on his feet and the window was wide open.

The coat he was wearing wasn't his. It

was three sizes too big and it had been given to him by a dinosaur. Well not a dinosaur exactly, a Dinotek…

Marlin rolled over and rubbed his head.

However could he explain all this to anyone?

It was all so amazing, so incredible, they'd think he was making it up.

They would laugh!

Or worse, they might scream. Because they might think the Dinoteks were dangerous…

Marlin sat up.

Dangerous…

He had suddenly remembered something very important from last night.

He jumped out of bed.

He had to get help – and there was only one person in the world who would listen.

****

Marlin sprinted down the back garden and along the alleyway between the houses.

There, tucked away among a tangle of

bushes was a little brick building with a patched-up metal roof. It was Uncle Gus' workshop.

It was built against the side of an oak tree and a tyre hung from a rope that was looped over one of the tree's branches. Marlin and Uncle Gus had tied it up there last summer and he had spent lazy afternoons swinging from it, reading.

No time for reading now though…

As he sprinted along the alley Marlin was glad to hear hammering sounds from inside the little building. Uncle Gus was in.

****

The old man sat quietly as Marlin told his whole story. He nodded from time to time but didn't speak.

They were perched together on the sofa and Uncle Gus was sipping from a big mug of tea. Steam curled up through his bushy eyebrows and made him look like a wizard.

Marlin was holding a mug of tea as well but he was too busy talking to drink anything.

He told Uncle Gus how the Dinoteks had finally come back to life.

He grabbed a sheet of paper and drew a sketch to show just how impressive the T-Rex was.

Uncle Gus leaned forwards and added some notes of his own to the picture as Marlin talked. He was very interested in machines.

"Yes, yes, I can see he'd be fast this one… it's a nice design, lad, very nice… and what's this?"

He pointed to the creature's back. Marlin nodded. That was the best thing of all!

The T-Rex had a special, hidden seat on his back. And last night the creature

15

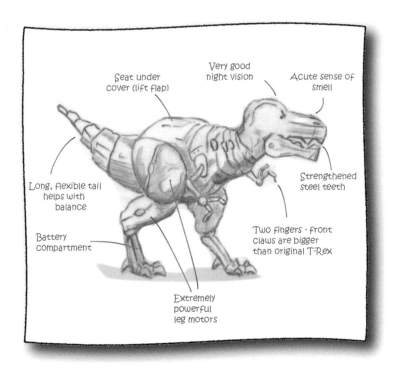

Seat under cover (lift flap)

Very good night vision

Acute sense of smell

Long, flexible tail helps with balance

Strengthened steel teeth

Battery compartment

Two fingers - front claws are bigger than original T-Rex

Extremely powerful leg motors

had picked him up in its teeth, flipped him through the air, and caught him very carefully so he'd landed right next to the seat.

"It's very safe and you can ride on him. It's like… like the world's best roller coaster!"

"Ah! That sounds fabulous lad, I do love a good roller coaster. I remember there used to be one down at the sea front. Lovely mechanism it had…"

16

Marlin's face changed.

"But Uncle, there's trouble too. The museum manager hates the Dinoteks – he wants to destroy them and turn them into scrap metal. I've done my best to help but Protos is still asleep and I don't know what to do next…"

Marlin waited to see what his uncle would say.

Uncle Gus had put down his mug and was pacing up and down, frowning.

Marlin looked up at him.

"What do you think, Uncle?"

Uncle Gus stopped pacing – and suddenly headed for the back of his workshop.

"Two things lad," he called. "Two things…"

His voice was muffled because now he was rummaging inside a cupboard.

He emerged, holding a rucksack.

"First, I think you are about to have a very important adventure."

He passed Marlin the rucksack.

"I had this packed for you, just in case. I've put in some tools, some food and – Ah!"

Suddenly he clapped his hand to his head. "I nearly forgot!"

He dashed over to his workbench and grabbed a golden box to give Marlin.

"The battery charger!" said Marlin.

"Exactly, lad! Just in case the Dinoteks run low. About twenty minutes for each battery should be enough."

Marlin stuffed the golden box into the rucksack.

"What's the second thing?" he asked.

"Eh?"

"You said there were two things Uncle!"

"Did I? Ah yes! The second thing is this lad – you need a *plan*."

****

Five minutes later Marlin saw something that he'd never seen before, and never really thought that he ever would.

Uncle Gus pushed his old car out of the workshop and started up the engine.

It had been in there for so long, in pieces, that Marlin didn't think it would ever actually work.

But it did.

The engine chugged a bit at first, but then it settled into a steady, rumbling purr.

Marlin grinned. It was a great sound!

They jumped into the car and headed for the museum.

Chapter Two

· · · · · · · · · · · · · · · ·

The Creature on
the Lawn

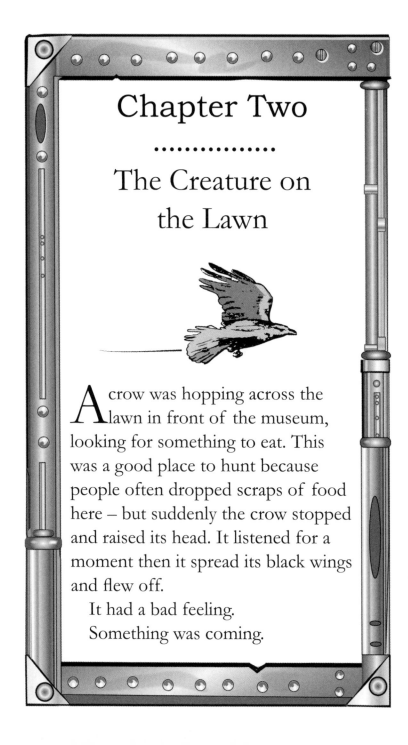

A crow was hopping across the lawn in front of the museum, looking for something to eat. This was a good place to hunt because people often dropped scraps of food here – but suddenly the crow stopped and raised its head. It listened for a moment then it spread its black wings and flew off.

It had a bad feeling.

Something was coming.

A minute later another creature arrived. It looked around warily, checking for danger, then it hurried across the grass to stand under a tree.

This was a good place to hide.

From here you could look across the open square to the museum and see everything that was going on.

And today, a lot would be happening here.

The creature was fully grown and quite large.

Its name was Oliver Grubbler.

Grubbler was the museum manager.

He lifted a pair of binoculars to his eyes and scanned the building.

Nothing. No sign of life.

But Grubbler wasn't fooled. He knew they were in there somewhere.

He thought about moving closer but decided not to. The Dinoteks must not see him. When the attack on the museum began – very soon now – it had to be a total surprise.

"Mr Grubbler!" called a voice.

He looked up to see a man in a grey suit hurrying across the lawn towards him. It was the Mayor.

"Have you seen them again? Have you seen the monsters?"

"Not yet," whispered Grubbler.

The Mayor glanced at the museum. He was sweating nervously. He pulled out a tissue and wiped his brow.

"And you're sure? The monsters are definitely in there?"

"I'm certain," Grubbler replied. "They're hiding inside. But they won't be able to hide for long. Not

23

once my friends get here…"

And at exactly that moment, as the museum clock struck ten, Howard H. Snickenbacker and his Demolition Army arrived.

****

Snickenbacker's Demolition Army appeared like this: the first thing to arrive was a truck.

Just a truck. There was nothing unusual about it, except for its colour. It was completely black, from the top of its cabin to the bottom of its chunky wheels.

Next came a jeep and there was nothing very odd about that either except that it was bigger than usual and also totally black.

But the things that came after, well they were *very* strange.

Some of the vehicles looked like diggers, and others like bulldozers, but most were strange mix-up machines with lots of odd pieces joined together. They had hooks and chains and gigantic snapping claws.

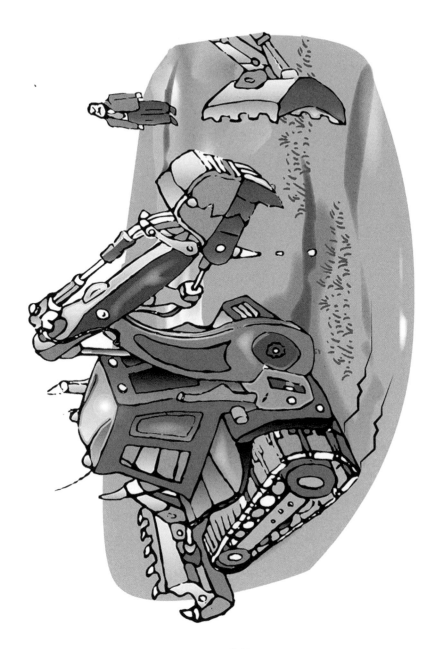

All of them were painted the same shiny black and, as they came into the square one after another, they looked like a colony of gigantic, lumbering beetles.

Grubbler watched them roll forwards and he smiled as he felt the air rumbling and roaring. It was a good sound. A powerful sound.

They crunched their way across the road, then trundled up onto the lawn in front of the museum and began to line up in rows.

The Mayor looked anxiously at the neat grass and the beautiful flower beds as the wheels rolled over them.

"Oh dear…I hope they don't make too much mess Mr Grubbler…"

But Grubbler wasn't listening. He was staring through his binoculars again waiting for the attack on the museum to begin.

Neither Grubbler nor the Mayor noticed when one small vehicle arrived late.

****

Uncle Gus parked by the edge of the grass.

"It looks like we're just in time lad…"

In front of them the black trucks and diggers were still lining up. Uncle Gus tutted and shook his head.

"Just look at them all…"

"Don't worry, I'll get past them Uncle!"

Marlin heaved the rucksack from the back seat and slipped it onto his back.

"You know what to do lad?"

"Yes," said Marlin.

"Ready?"

"Ready!" – and he gave his uncle a hug before opening the door and jumping out.

A moment later Uncle Gus revved up the little car's engine. He drove up onto the grass and began chugging around in circles, weaving in and out among the neat rows of diggers. The drivers in their black uniforms looked at him, puzzled. Some of them began to shout at him but Uncle Gus just honked his horn and waved cheerfully.

Round and round he went.

Marlin took his chance.

While everyone was looking the other way he set off across the grass towards the museum.

He walked very calmly – *just look as if you belong here* – and nobody noticed him. He got right across the lawn and ducked into the side road next to the museum.

Easy, he grinned.

Now he just had to work out how to get inside.

Chapter Three

The Only Way In

Marlin sneaked into the road beside the museum and looked up at the impressive stone building. One of the windows was open.

He was certain that he could squeeze through it. But first he had to reach it. It was on the first floor.

The front of the museum was very beautiful. It was covered with carvings of plants and animals. But on this side of the building there were no ornaments, nothing to hang on to.

Except for one thing – a crooked cast-iron drainpipe was fixed to the wall. As it snaked upwards, it went close to the window. It looked sturdy enough to climb.

Marlin looked at it.

High up, there were connections running out from the sides of the pipe like branches from a tree. And climbing trees was easy.

Marlin smiled.

But at that moment a large man in a uniform came lumbering towards him.

****

It was Buster Crank the security guard. Buster was a big man and he swayed from side to side as he walked. But he hadn't noticed Marlin. No, he was thinking about the mysterious events of last night.

Last night.

Hmmm…

He scratched his head and tried to work it out.

Something very odd had happened to Buster while he was guarding the Glass Tower. First there had been the strange silver thing – he had seen it, he had definitely seen it. And then there was the clever thief.

Yes. Buster had got into big trouble over that. Mr Grubbler had shouted at him.

Somehow a thief had got past him and into the building.

But how had that happened?

Buster pondered.

And then he looked up and noticed Marlin walking towards him. The boy had a heavy bag on his back and his hands were stuffed into his pockets.

He didn't *look* like a criminal – but today Buster had to be especially careful.

"What are you up to?" he demanded.

"I was just wondering," replied the boy.

"Wondering what?"

And the boy pointed upwards, above Buster's head.

"Should that window be open? I mean, couldn't someone get in?"

Buster looked up.

"You're right!"

He stretched up, but couldn't reach the window. He jumped, but didn't get very far.

Too many sausages this morning Buster, he thought.

"That's no use," said the boy, shaking his head. "Would you like me to help?"

Buster looked at him.

"Would you?"

The boy nodded.

"See that drainpipe? Give me a hand up. I'm sure I could climb it."

"A good plan," nodded Buster.

He knelt on one knee and helped the boy to clamber up.

The boy was quick. He shimmied up the drainpipe to reach the window.

"Careful!" called Buster.

"OK," said the boy as he pulled himself onto the ledge. "Nearly there…"

Then he disappeared through the window and – BANG – he shut it from inside.

Buster nodded, satisfied. Now the building was totally secure.

He carried on his patrol, along the road, and as he went he smiled.

Nobody would get past him today.

33

Chapter Four

· · · · · · · · · · · · · ·

Friends
Meet Again

Marlin sprinted through the empty corridors and his footsteps echoed in the silence. The museum was deserted now but he knew that it would soon be full of people. In his mind he pictured the Dinoteks being surrounded and dragged outside in chains. Even Flame, with his legs tangled, would be pulled down and taken.

No! That must not happen!

He sprang down a staircase three steps at a time, ran into the museum entrance hall and crashed straight into the T-Rex.

"Woah!"

Flame looked down amazed.

"Marlin! What are you doing here? You're supposed to be at home!"

"I came to find *you*," replied Marlin, picking himself up. "Why did you leave me behind? I told you, I'm going to help you!"

The T-Rex snorted and shook his head.

"It's kind of you to try but what I really need here is another T-Rex. Or a whole family of them…"

And he looked out through the glass doors. All morning he had been watching as the black vehicles got closer. Now a massive bulldozer had rumbled up with smoke billowing from its exhaust pipe.

"I'm sure it won't be long now," he muttered to himself. "They're moving in…"

"But where's Protos?" exclaimed Marlin. "And all the others?"

"Upstairs," answered Flame. "They're still trying to wake Protos but it's not working."

He sighed and shook his head.

"I think there must be something wrong with his battery. Marlin, do you think – Marlin?!"

But Marlin had already gone.

Steg couldn't think of what to do next.
He could see the others watching him
– Dacky and the little ones – and he knew
how much they wanted Protos to wake up.
He wanted it too.

"I'll just try it one more time the other
way," he said.

"But you've already tried that three
times!" squeaked Siggy.

"I know!" snapped Steg. "But what else
can I do? It doesn't help with everyone
staring at me!"

Siggy hung his head and Steg immediately

felt bad.

"I'm sorry," he said. "I'm doing my best."

He reached into Protos' battery space – the compartment in his leg – and pulled the grey cylinder out again. He turned it over in his beak and pushed it back in, snapping the cover shut.

Nothing happened.

They all looked again at the old Centrosaurus. But there was no sign of life, none at all.

Chapter Five

············

The Attack of the Demolition Army

"It's time," growled Grubbler. Howard H. Snickenbacker was standing next to him on the museum steps, looking up at the glass doors.

Nothing moved. The air was still. Even the birds had stopped singing.

"Are you sure?" asked Snickenbacker.

"Yes," nodded Grubbler.

"Excellent. Then let's begin."

****

Marlin skidded into the secret room. "The battery!" he shouted. "Put it in!"

Steg looked up.

"I did! It's not working!"

"It has to!"

Marlin dashed over and fell to his knees beside Protos' huge foot. His eyes scanned across the mechanical parts, desperately searching for the problem.

He remembered the very first day when he had accidentally brought the old creature back to life.

It was the first time he'd realised the Dinoteks were living machines. All he had done was fix a few loose parts – without even thinking. It had been so easy.

But now he felt panicked and he couldn't see at all what to do.

The battery was in its right place. There were no loose wires. There was one pin hanging out and he snapped it back, but that made no difference.

Then suddenly he heard the sound that he had been dreading. The sound of roaring engines from the front of the building.

"They're coming!" he exclaimed.

Steg snorted and his armour plates bristled angrily.

"We've got to help Flame! We must defend ourselves!"

And with a flick of his spear-covered tail he led the way to the door. Dacky and the Troodons went with him.

Marlin followed too.

He looked back one last time at Protos then he sprinted after the others towards the entrance hall where Flame was alone, facing the attack.

Chapter Six

·················

The Bulldozer

In a billow of smoke the massive bulldozer trundled up to the museum steps. It paused at the top.

Behind it, the others also came forwards, their engines revving. A digger lifted its black jaws – black, except for two rows of steel-grey teeth. They snapped hungrily in the air.

Oliver Grubbler lifted a megaphone to his mouth.

"Dinosaurs! Listen to me! You are ordered to leave the building immediately!"

His voice echoed harshly above the roar of the machines.

"You have one minute to surrender! Come out NOW or you will be destroyed!"

Then he began the countdown.

"Fifty nine…fifty eight…fifty seven…"

******

Inside the entrance hall Flame moved at last. He turned and stepped forwards.

Now he was standing directly in front of the doors and he could see that he was badly outnumbered. If he could just hold the first machine back – the bulldozer at the front – he might be able to block the way.

If...

The black machine looked strong. Flame was built for speed and he had powerful jaws but the bulldozer was made to push and to shove.

It would not stop.

Its caterpillar tracks would grip the ground firmly but Flame's clawed feet would scrape and slip on the polished tiles as he tried to hold his place.

He would be pushed backwards and then all the other machines would come in one after the other. They would surround him and attack together.

He knew this would happen unless he could think of something else to do.

Unless...

"We're here!" barked a voice behind him.

Steg powered into the hall.

******

The Stegosaurus' armour plates were shivering fiercely and his eyes flashed. Flame thought he looked suddenly bigger.

"Where do you want me?!" Steg snapped.

"Here," answered Flame, nodding to the empty space next to him.

The smaller Dinoteks crowded in now – Dacky, Comp, Siggy – and they made a second line behind the two giants.

And then Marlin skidded into the room. He looked around frantically.

What could he do to help?

Suddenly he saw what he needed!

There was a suit of armour next to the ticket desk and Marlin grabbed its shield. He took the sword too and lifted it above his head – it was long and heavy but felt good in his hand – then he went to stand in-between Flame and Steg.

Flame looked down at him, sternly.

"Marlin! You can't stand there, you might get hurt!" he growled.

"Yes. That's a bad idea. Very bad indeed," said another voice.

It took all of them a moment to recognise who it was. Then they turned – Marlin, Flame and the others – to see Protos standing right behind them.

****

"Those bulldozers can be a bit rough," Protos said. "I wouldn't get in their way if I were you."

He turned and lumbered through a doorway at the back of the hall.

For a moment nobody moved – so amazed were they to see him that they even forgot about the people outside.

But then Grubbler's voice boomed louder.

"…twenty…nineteen…eighteen…"

Marlin shook himself.

"Come on everyone!"

He ran to catch up with Protos and the others all followed.

"You're back!" he exclaimed. "You're awake!"

"Yes and I'm so pleased to see you," the old creature chuckled.

Suddenly he stopped.

"Did you get into trouble with your teacher?"

Teacher? What was he talking about?!

Then Marlin remembered his school trip all those weeks ago. Protos had been asleep since then!

"No, I didn't get into trouble," he said.

"Oh that *is* a relief," nodded Protos.

And he set off again.

"I'm so glad everything's OK."

"But Protos you don't understand, they're going to…"

"You know I was quite worried about you. I thought you might get told off for being late. I remember once when – "

"Protos! Listen!"

The Centrosaurus stopped and turned to him.

"Wait a moment Marlin," he whispered. "First there's something important I need to tell you. Don't tell the others, I don't want to frighten them…"

"What is it?"

"All those bulldozers and diggers, did you notice them? I can't be totally sure but I think – I think they're planning something bad…"

"I know!" exclaimed Marlin. "That's what I've been trying to tell you! They're attacking us!"

"Really?"

"Yes!"

"Oh."

At that moment there was a loud crash behind them and the sound of glass shattering.

"Quick Protos, you've got to do something!"

Protos blinked and looked thoughtful for a moment. Then he nodded.

"You'd better follow me then…"

Chapter Seven

·················

A Room Full of Dinosaur Books

Now Protos moved surprisingly quickly.

He hurried through a series of long galleries, picking his way between display cabinets and exhibits.

They went through Dacky's favourite part of the museum, the Flight Gallery, and then headed down a long corridor.

Suddenly he stopped again.

"This is the best place to hide."

Marlin looked around. They were in a room full of books. On one wall there was a huge map of the world showing where different fossils had been found.

Steg pushed his way to the front.

"This isn't clever. We'll be trapped here!"

Flame nodded.

"He's right, it's not safe."

As he said it, they heard more crashing sounds. The Troodons huddled together and Dacky shook his wings.

"Don't worry, I won't be long," replied Protos.

And to Marlin's surprise, he began looking through the books.

There were thousands of them, mostly old and dusty.

"Let me see now... *Lost Giants of the Triassic*...I enjoyed that one, especially chapter ten...*Creatures of the Arctic Forest* ... very good but a bit chilly ...*The Great Cakes Cookery Book*, hmm...well that shouldn't be in here at all... Ah, here we are – *Secrets of the Jurassic Mountain*."

He looked up at them all and his eyes shone.

"It's a wonderful place, the Jurassic Mountain!"

He took hold of the book with his metal beak and pulled it. There was a scraping

sound and Marlin jumped backwards. The big wall map was moving!

It slid to one side. And behind it was a hidden passage sloping down into the dark.

Marlin peered inside and felt cool air on his face.

"Where does it go Protos?"

But before he could say any more Flame interrupted.

"Quick! They're here! The people are coming!"

Shouts echoed through the hall and then came the sound of heavy boots running towards them.

"Follow me now!" said Protos.

And he led them into the passage.

****

The wall map slid shut again – CLICK! – and then everything went black.

"Well that's a relief," the old creature said. "You know I wondered if it would still work…"

"But what now?" squawked Dacky.

One of the Troodons gave a frightened squeak.

"First things first," whispered Protos. "Are you there Steg? Can you give us some light?"

For a moment nothing happened, then Marlin saw the most magical sight.

The dark passage was filled with a sparkling light as the Stegosaurus began to glow. His towering armour plates were suddenly illuminated in gold and blue. The long spikes on his tail were shining bright red.

"Wow!" gasped the Troodons. "That's so

cool!"

"Steg, that's brilliant!" exclaimed Marlin. "I didn't know you could do that!"

"It's a defensive trick," sniffed Steg. "Ancient stegosaurs probably did something similar."

"It's a good trick," beamed Protos. "And just the thing to help us now."

Then he lumbered forwards ahead of them into the gloom.

****

The passage wound downwards, twisting and turning. Down and down they went. It was long and narrow and they had to walk single file.

This was easy for Marlin, the Troodons and Dacky.

But the big Dinoteks had trouble. Steg's armour plates scraped along the passage roof. And coming behind the others, right at the back, Flame could only just squeeze himself through.

He closed his eyes and tried not to think about it too much. T-Rexs didn't like being closed in.

"Not far now," called Protos. "Keep going!"

And sure enough they soon came out into a wide, underground room. The walls were made with little bricks that looked very old. Marlin could see boxes and crates stretching away into the shadows.

"Here we are. Come in everyone," called Protos. "Welcome to the Underground Stores!"

Marlin watched the Dinoteks come crowding in. They gathered round in a group, all talking at once and telling Protos their news. The Troodons couldn't keep still, they were scampering around (and underneath) the big Dinoteks and they even started jumping across Steg's tail.

Marlin smiled. But it wasn't long before his smile faded.

Somewhere far above them he thought he heard rumbling sounds.

Chapter Eight

· · · · · · · · · · · · · · ·

Gone!

The Demolition Army swarmed through the museum like angry ants. The bulldozer smashed its way into the entrance hall, destroying the glass door. And then dozens of black uniformed figures came scurrying in, clambering over the rubble and broken glass.

They found no dinosaurs.

Snickenbacker strode into the hall and Grubbler stomped in after him with a fierce grin on his face. He was looking forward to seeing the Dinoteks tied up in chains.

"Where are they?" he demanded.

"Hiding of course," said Snickenbacker.

Grubbler snorted angrily but

Snickenbacker laughed.

"Don't worry. We'll find them."

Then he turned to his people, and gave the order.

"Let's hunt!"

Immediately the black figures spread out and began moving through the halls. They would search all of the rooms one by one, pulling everything apart.

They had done this before and they were good at it.

The bulldozers rolled in too. They lowered their scoops and began shoving exhibits out of the way. They were making the path clear for the even bigger machines coming in behind.

"There may be some mess," smiled Snickenbacker as one of the glass cabinets was crunched up against the wall. "I'm afraid it can't be avoided."

Most museum managers would have cared about that. But Oliver Grubbler didn't. At that moment his mind was filled with only one thing.

"Just catch the dinosaurs!" he snarled.

And while everyone was rushing around, far above on the old stone walls, the carvings of animals looked down. There were creatures of all kinds, and delicate plants, curling and climbing upwards. This museum had been their home for over a hundred years – and they were only statues, not really alive.

But you could almost imagine them feeling sad at all the destruction below.

****

"I see…yes…Oh dear…"

Protos listened for a long time while Marlin and the Dinoteks told him about everything that had happened – about Grubbler and Snickenbacker, the Mayor and Inspector Bailey, the kind police detective.

Flame told him about Marlin's adventure in the Glass Tower.

"…biscuits, eh?! That was a good trick! I would never have thought of it…"

And when Marlin got to the part about the scrap metal plan Steg's armour plates bristled. That made the light in the room shimmer and all their shadows danced. Siggy squeaked and huddled next to Comp.

"Don't be frightened," Protos said to them. "We're all safe down here."

"But for how long?" said Steg. "We can't stay here forever. In the end we'll have to go out and fight."

Flame growled.

"Don't worry, we can beat them."

But Protos shook his head.

"Do you remember the Professor's Three Golden Rules?" he said gently.

They looked at each other and then Comp squeaked: "Where *is* the Professor? Will we see him soon?"

"Sshh!" said Flame. "Let Protos tell us the Three Golden Rules."

"One," said Protos. "We must always look after each other."

They all nodded.

"Two, we must never hurt anybody…"

They all shook their heads.

"And three, if somebody needs help we should always try to help them."

The Dinoteks nodded solemnly again.

Marlin could tell that they had all heard these rules before.

Then Protos sighed.

"And as for the Professor… I'm afraid we were all asleep for ages. Years in fact. I think the Professor must have died a long time ago."

The two little Troodons nodded – but they looked confused.

The older Dinoteks understood though and they hung their heads sadly.

"So now we're on our own," sighed Steg.

"No we're not! We have Marlin to help us now," said Protos. "He is very clever you know and brave too – although he *will* have to go home soon."

"Not before I've made sure you're all safe," said Marlin firmly.

Protos frowned but didn't reply.

He lumbered across the room into the shadows.

"There's something the Professor left for us…"

He reached down with his beak and picked something up. Then he laid it down at their feet. It was a long shape, bundled up in a cloth.

"Will you carry it, Flame? Very gently?"

"Yes," said the T-Rex solemnly.

He picked the bundle up, turned and laid it into the hatch on his back.

"Now let's just keep ourselves hidden underground for a bit longer," said Protos. "We can have a nice rest. Then as soon as it's dark outside it will be safe to leave."

The Dinoteks settled down and closed their eyes. And while they rested Marlin opened his rucksack. He took out the power charger and went round to all of them.

He attached the clips to each battery, just as Uncle Gus had said, and one at a time he powered them up.

He powered himself up too – in the rucksack he found a nice heap of sandwiches.

****

The sun was setting in front of the museum and the Demolition Army was fading into the shadows. As it grew darker

their strange black shapes became hard to see. And then, one by one, their headlights flicked on. They shone like eyes.

Grubbler was standing on the museum steps with his hands stuffed into his pockets. The Mayor was standing with him and for once he wasn't totally grey. There was a pink colour in his cheeks.

"The City Council will not be happy Grubbler," he tutted. "All this mess, all this damage. But there were no dinosaurs!"

The Mayor looked across at the flower beds, now trampled and churned. And he hadn't even seen the mess inside the museum yet!

"There were dinosaurs! I mean there *are* dinosaurs!" protested Grubbler. "They're just hiding…"

"He's right."

Snickenbacker came striding out, holding something in his hand.

"Look what we've found," he smiled. "There's a room full of old maps in there and my people discovered something very interesting."

The Mayor frowned.

"A map?"

"Not quite, but nearly," said Snickenbacker. "It's a plan. A plan of the museum."

He unfolded the paper.

"Now," he said, running his finger across

the old drawing. "It seems that this building has some secrets, Mr Grubbler."

"What do you mean?"

"There is a passage. It's shown on this plan but we can't find the door."

"A secret passage?" gasped the Mayor.

"Exactly," smiled Snickenbacker. "*That* is how the dinosaurs got away."

Grubbler clapped his hands together and his smile returned.

"So all we have to do is find the way in!"

He snatched the plan and spread it out on the ground. The Mayor knelt down beside him and they began to study it. But Snickenbacker laughed.

"We can be much cleverer than that," he said. "Don't look for the way in – look for the way out. That's where we'll catch them."

Chapter Nine

•••••••••••••••

On the Run

"I think it's time to go," whispered Protos.

"Yes, I'm ready," said Marlin. He stood up and heaved the rucksack onto his back.

The Dinoteks shook themselves awake. Flame yawned and Dacky spread his wings, stretching across the whole room.

One of the little Troodons came over and sniffed at Marlin.

"Hello again Comp," Marlin smiled, patting its head.

The Troodon giggled.

"I'm Siggy," he squeaked, and ran off.

****

One by one they left the store room and headed along a tunnel. At the end was a door made of thick steel plates riveted together. It was rusty and Marlin guessed that it hadn't been opened for years. But it must have been well made because Protos pushed against it and it swung open with barely a creak.

They came out into a narrow cobbled street. It was already dark.

"Quietly now," whispered the Centrosaurus. "And Steg, you'd better turn off your lights."

Marlin looked both ways, up and down the street. There was a faint evening mist, making the street lights look soft and smudged. There was nobody in sight, nothing moving.

"We can't stay here," Marlin hissed.

Protos nodded.

"Yes, you're right," he said. "We must go north!"

Then he hesitated.

"Um, do you know which way north is?"

Marlin frowned and pointed up the road.

"I don't know – maybe that way?"

"Good!"

Protos heaved himself round.

"This way everyone, quickly."

And he lumbered along the road. The others followed him. Marlin carefully shut the metal door and ran after them.

They kept in the shadows close to the wall. There was a street lamp ahead, spreading a pool of light onto the road. One after another they hurried under it – their metal skins flashing as they passed –

then quickly got back into the dark.

Protos stopped. They had reached the end of the street.

"Marlin you were right," he beamed. "We came the right way. I remember this road!"

In front of them was a main road. It was wide and brightly lit. As they stood there, a line of cars sped by.

"But if we go out there we'll be spotted!" Flame growled.

"We'll be quick," replied Protos. "We must get across to the other side."

He pointed with his horn. Over the road there was a dark gap between the buildings.

"You go first Flame. Go up that path. Get to the very end and we'll all meet there."

"OK."

The T-Rex looked up and down the road, he sniffed the air – then leapt forwards and was across in no more than three strides. The Troodons scampered after him.

"Your turn Steg!"

Steg grumbled – he wasn't happy leaving the museum – but when he set off he was

very quick. He dashed across the road and disappeared into the shadows after Flame.

More cars passed. They waited.

"Now us!" said Protos.

Dacky went first, flapping and hopping, with Marlin close after him.

Protos followed. He was slower than all the others – one of his back legs dragged when he tried to run – but he pushed on as fast as he could.

And he got to the other side not a moment too soon.

Protos was only just disappearing into the dark when a sinister black truck came speeding into the narrow street behind him.

****

Grubbler jumped out of the vehicle, still clutching the museum plan.

He looked up and down the road, then spotted the rusty door.

"There!"

He sprinted over to it and pressed his ear up against the cold metal.

"What are you doing?" asked

72

Snickenbacker.

"Listening of course! It's an old hunter's trick. I'll be able to hear them before they come out. And then – "

But Snickenbacker chuckled.

"You're too late. They've already gone."

"Gone? How can you know that?!"

Snickenbacker pointed at the ground. At first Grubbler couldn't see anything, but then he noticed some rusty metal flakes scattered across the pavement.

"That door has just been opened," said Snickenbacker. "And look there."

He pointed along the road. There was a paving stone, cracked and slightly lifted. There were little fragments of stone and grit scattered around it that had not yet blown away. Something heavy had pressed on it, and cracked it, very recently.

Snickenbacker turned on his heels and walked back to the car. Grubbler hurried after him.

"So what do we do now?"

But Snickenbacker was already on his phone.

"Smith? We've found their trail. They're heading north. Get all the hunters moving. I want every road out of the city watched."

He snapped off the phone then turned back to Grubbler.

"They think they've got away but they've made a big mistake," he said. "They're in the open, they're too big to hide and they can't leave the city!"

****

Marlin followed Dacky up the path as it climbed uphill, winding between bushes and trees. It was quite wide – wide enough for a car to come along – but it was stony and full of pot-holes, not like a proper road. There were no street lights here and Marlin had to be careful not to trip.

"I can't see Protos yet," he said, looking over his shoulder.

"Don't worry boy, he'll come," cawed Dacky.

When he walked, the Pterosaur half

hopped and half flapped. His wings
brushed against the bushes.

"I'd rather be flying," he said. "But of
course I don't want to leave you."

"It was good flying last night," said
Marlin. "Thanks again for saving me!"

"Oh, don't mention it," said Dacky. "It
was nothing, really…"

But in the dark Marlin could tell that the
Pterosaur was pleased.

Marlin looked behind again.

"Dacky, do you think we should wait?"

"No, let's get to the top. Protos will find us."

They hurried on – but Marlin kept glancing backwards.

The path was becoming narrower and soon Dacky had to fold in his wings and walk without using them at all. That made him a lot slower.

Now, with trees all around them, it was much darker too.

Marlin stumbled.

But then Dacky stopped and whispered.

"Look ahead boy, there's a light!"

Marlin could see it, a faint glow shining red beneath the trees.

"It's Steg," he exclaimed. "He's lighting the way for us!"

****

In the street beside the museum Snickenbacker snapped off his phone and walked around to the back of his truck.

"What's happening now?" demanded Grubbler.

"My hunting squad is in position. Every

route out of the city is blocked."

Snickenbacker swung open the car boot and leaned inside.

And when he stood up again Grubbler saw that he was holding some sort of weapon. It was long, like a rifle, but with two strange cylinders fixed to the barrel.

"Now comes the good part," said Snickenbacker. "Now we make our first catch!"

And he strode down the road, heading north, with Grubbler scurrying after him.

****

The Dinoteks were huddled together under a tree. They had followed the path as far as it would go and now the way ahead was tangled and overgrown.

"Where now?" hissed Steg. "This is a dead end, we'll have to turn back!"

Marlin stood anxiously looking behind. Then finally Protos lumbered into view.

"Well done," he puffed. "Is everyone here?"

"Yes, we're all here!" whispered Marlin.

The Centrosaurus glanced over his shoulder, back down the path. He seemed to be listening to something.

"I think we'd better move on," he said. "No time to rest. Flame, there should be a small path just through the bushes. It's quite steep, but not very long."

Flame nodded.

"I'll find it."

And Marlin heard the undergrowth cracking and crunching as the T-Rex pushed through it.

"Follow behind Flame everyone."

They moved forwards in a line and Steg kept a faint light glowing to help show the way. Marlin walked beside Protos again.

"But where are we going?" he whispered.

"To a safe place I hope, Marlin," replied the old creature. "I came up here many years ago. The Professor showed me. I just hope I've remembered it correctly."

He glanced backwards again, listening.

"We need to be quick, I think…"

But before he could explain there was a crashing sound in the bushes ahead and Flame re-appeared.

"Protos! We can't go this way!" he hissed.

"Why not? What's wrong Flame?" demanded Steg.

"There's a creature!" exclaimed the T-Rex. "A gigantic metal snake!"

Chapter Ten
········

The Gigantic Snake

"Good heavens!" exclaimed Protos. "Let me see!"

And he hurried ahead. Marlin watched anxiously as he heaved himself up the steep bank.

A giant snake? Where did *that* come from?

At the top, Protos nudged very slowly forwards and peeped through the bushes. Then suddenly Marlin heard him laugh.

"It's OK, the snake is friendly! Come up here everyone, quickly."

They scrambled after him to the top of the bank.

"Look there," he said. "Can you see it?"

Marlin peered through the trees.

There was an open space and in the moonlight he could see the creature that Flame had spotted.

It was lying there with its long black body, totally still. Waiting in ambush? It stretched away into the distance. It really was huge...

But suddenly Marlin laughed too.

"It's not a snake!"

"What is it then?" frowned Flame.

"A train!"

Protos led them all forwards.

"Oh, yes of course," muttered Flame, embarrassed. "I should have thought of that."

"What's a train?" hissed Steg.

The Troodons shook their heads. They didn't know either.

"We could ask Professor Marlin," squeaked Comp.

"He's not a Professor," snorted Steg.

Then they followed after the others.

****

The Dinoteks gathered together by the railway track and stared up at the goods train parked in front of them.

It was long, with high, closed wagons at the front and a line of open, flat carriages at the back.

It wasn't moving, but Marlin could hear the whir and click of its motors. He looked down the line and saw a red light.

A red signal.

That's why the train had stopped.

"It will go as soon as the light turns green," he whispered.

"Yes," nodded Protos. "I think we're just in time. We must all get on board."

"I can't get up there," protested Steg.

But Protos was looking behind again, peering anxiously into the dark.

"Hmmm...I think we should be quick," he said.

Straight away the two Troodons hopped up onto the nearest wagon.

"Come on Steg! It's easy!" squeaked Siggy.

Dacky flapped his wings twice, and was up beside them.

Protos looked at Marlin.

"Now you've helped us I think it's time for you to be getting home," he began. "Your teacher won't be happy if you are too tired for school and also there's a – "

But Marlin shook his head.

"I'm coming all the way!" he said firmly. "And don't worry about school, it's the holidays."

Before Protos could argue he scrambled up onto the train.

Steg was still hesitating

"I'll never get up there," he grumbled. "And neither will you Protos!"

"Yes you will. Both of you," grunted Flame.

He was dragging something towards them in his jaws – a massive fallen tree trunk. He dropped it right next to the track.

"Up you go Steg!"

The armoured creature snorted impatiently – but he clambered up on to the trunk and began balancing along it. At last he got his front feet onto the edge of the wagon and gave a mighty heave. He was up!

"Well done!" cawed Dacky.

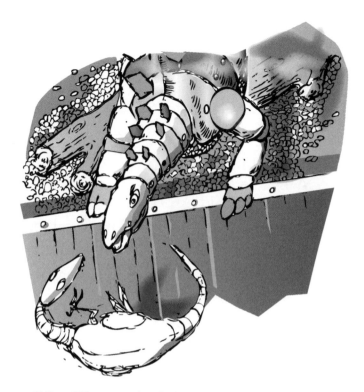

"Cool!" squeaked the Troodons.

Steg bristled.

"It wasn't hard."

Now Flame dragged the tree trunk along
to the next wagon.

"Your turn Protos!"

"Thank you," said the old creature.

He copied Steg, balancing in the same
way, and got his front feet onto the wagon.
But suddenly Marlin shouted a warning.

"The signal! It's green!"

There was a heavy clunk and the train started to move.

Protos didn't have the strength for the jump. He clung onto the wagon, but his back legs slipped off the tree trunk and dragged along in the gravel.

He couldn't hold on!

Just before he fell, he had time to call out one last thing.

"Look after each other…find somewhere to hide… I'll come to you!"

The train lurched forwards.

The wheels turned faster, faster.

Protos fell – but then suddenly he felt himself rising again. He was actually floating up onto the wagon! He looked down and realised that Flame was pushing him up with his powerful head. There was a grinding of metal and the T-Rex groaned with the great effort of lifting such a weight.

"That's it! Come on! Come on!" he grunted.

And suddenly Protos was safely on board. Flame had done it!

Protos turned to say thank you – but even

at that moment Flame himself stumbled.

His claws slipped in the gravel and he crashed over.

"Flame!" shouted Marlin – and the others called out too.

They watched in horror as the great Dinotek struggled to stand while the train gathered speed and rattled away into the night.

Chapter Eleven

Flame Alone

Flame stood up again and shook himself. He turned to see the train disappearing. And then two men stepped out in front of him.

The big one he recognised. He was the man who had been standing in front of the museum all day. The man who had shouted into the megaphone.

The T-Rex sniffed at him. He knew the scent. It was Oliver Grubbler, their enemy.

The other man – the thin one – stepped forwards.

He lifted something, and smiled. There was a sound – BANG! – and something shot through the air.

Flame looked down,

puzzled. A net was tangled around his legs.

BANG!

Now there was another net. It was covering his head. He shook it, but it wouldn't come off. That made the men laugh.

The big one, Grubbler, pointed at him.

"Not so scary now are you T-Rex?!"

Then he turned to his friend.

"Can I have a go?"

"Be my guest!"

BANG! BANG!

More nets. Flame was becoming tangled! Grubbler raised the gun above his head and shouted.

"I am Grubbler the Beast-Slayer!"

Then he fired three more shots and the nets began to wrap more tightly.

Flame looked at Grubbler.

Then he raised his head – stretched his jaws – and snapped the nets.

He straightened his legs and stepped forwards. More of the nets snapped. Finally, he shook himself and they all fell away, landing in a heap at his feet.

Both men stared at him, open mouthed, too astonished to even move.

Flame stared back at them.

The Second Golden Rule, we must never hurt anybody…

He turned and sprinted along the track.

****

How fast could an ancient T-Rex have run? Experts are still not sure.

But there's no doubt about Flame. He was fast, very fast.

If you'd been alive in the Cretaceous era

you might have been lucky enough to see something as good as this – or even *half* as good!

Flame came powering along the line faster than any creature in history.

He pounded forwards and the train came into view. He could see his friends. Now they were cheering for him, calling out his name.

He ran faster, head low, tail thrashing from side to side.

But the train was getting faster too.

It came around the bend – rattling and hissing – and onto the straight track. Then it began to pick up serious speed. Flame knew that it would soon accelerate beyond even his pace.

But he fixed his eyes ahead and pushed harder – *harder!* – he was *not* going to be left behind.

There was a moment when time seemed to stand still.

At that moment Flame and the train were going at exactly the same speed. A second later, and time would move on again, and then the train would pull away from him.

But just before that happened Flame threw himself forwards.

CRASH!

He landed on the last flat carriage.

It felt as though the wagon might be knocked off its rails. But it wasn't and Flame sat up, grinning.

"Do I need a ticket?"

Chapter Twelve

· · · · · · · · · · · · · · · ·

Follow the Dinosaurs!

Snickenbacker walked across to the broken nets. He reached down for one, held it up in his thin hands and looked closely at the ripped ends.

And to Grubbler's surprise he was smiling.

"Excellent!" he exclaimed.

"What do you mean?!" spluttered Grubbler. "They got away again and your net-gun didn't work!"

"My net-gun didn't work," replied Snickenbacker, taking his friend by the arm. "But I have other weapons that are much better. Wait till you see them Grubbler! And now at last I have found something worth hunting!"

He led Grubbler away from the railway line and they scrambled back down the steep path.

Snickenbacker pulled out his phone.

"Smith? Yes it's me. There's a railway line north of the museum. A train just left from here and the dinosaurs are on it. Find out where it's going!"

****

At the police headquarters, very close to the museum, Inspector Bailey was thinking about dinosaurs too.

Ever since her encounter with Grubbler yesterday, and her talk with Marlin, she'd been puzzling over it.

She had liked Marlin. The museum manager had called him a thief and that clearly wasn't true. But the boy's story had been very odd.

Dinoteks – machines coming to life – it couldn't really be true could it?

There was a knock on her door. A visitor…

The door opened and a man stepped in.

Almost without thinking about it Inspector Bailey noticed everything about his appearance – it was the habit of a police detective. He was in his sixties, early sixties probably. He had wild grey hair, dark eyes and a moustache.

He also had rough hands – so he was a builder maybe, or a mechanic?

Oil around the fingernails, a mechanic then…

He had a kind face.

"Please sit down. How can I help you?"

"Inspector, I need to find the dinosaurs."

"Well," she smiled. "You're not the only one. Today, everybody seems to be looking for them."

"Are you?"

"Actually no. It's not a police matter. No crime has been committed. And I'm not even convinced that these creatures exist – Mr?"

"Gus. They do exist. My nephew Marlin is with them."

Now Inspector Bailey was interested. She leaned forwards.

"Marlin Maxton? The boy who said he

could bring them to life?"

Him again...

"Yes, that's him, he's a great lad. He's helping the creatures. And they're called Dinoteks – they're not dangerous Inspector Bailey. They are perfectly safe."

"And you say Marlin is with them now Mr Gus? Is that wise?"

The old man scratched his head.

"I can't tell you why exactly. But I know the Dinoteks are good. They will look after Marlin, Inspector, I'm certain about that. And he'll look after them."

Inspector Bailey studied the man's face.

He was rather eccentric looking but he was honest.

"Well I'm glad you came to see me Mr Gus. Perhaps it is time the police got involved with this case…"

Yes, she thought, it was time she asked a few questions. All that disturbance at the museum…all those people running about in black uniforms! Something about this business wasn't right.

She didn't trust Oliver Grubbler –

and she definitely didn't like Howard Snickenbacker.

"Thank you for coming to see me Mr Gus. I'm going to investigate. I'll see what I can find out…"

She stood up.

"Do you know where the Dinoteks are now?"

"No. But I think they've got away somehow."

She sighed.

"Well, I only hope they've gone somewhere safe."

****

"Excellent! Get everyone there at once Smith – and make sure they're ready!"

Snickenbacker snapped off his phone and smiled at Grubbler.

"We've got them!"

"What do you mean?"

"In exactly one hour and twenty three minutes the train will be arriving at its last and only stop. When it does, my people will be there waiting."

Grubbler grinned.

"Now, shall we go back to my headquarters?" said Snickenbacker. "You can look at my Special Weapons while we wait for the good news!"

Chapter Thirteen

· · · · · · · · · · · · · · · ·

The Strange Star

The train was racing through the night at full speed and Marlin was huddled close to Protos, sheltering from the wind. He had his heavy coat pulled tightly around him.

The city was now far behind and so were their enemies. They had escaped.

But Protos looked worried.

"We have to get off," he frowned.

"What's wrong?"

"If we stay on this train we'll go too far. We need to go north, then west a bit."

Protos thought for a moment. Then he looked across at Dacky who was crouching on the next wagon, sheltering behind Steg.

"Dacky," he called. "Is it true? Can you really fly?"

****

Two minutes later Dacky was standing on the edge of the wagon, gripping it tight with his claws. He looked straight ahead, into the rushing wind. This could be dangerous…

His wings might be ripped off by the force of the air. Or he might lose control of his flight and crash to the ground.

He closed his eyes and counted to three.

Then he went.

WOOOOSH!

The speed of the train shot him upwards.

He felt his wings tug and strain. But he didn't crash… he soared!

It must have been like this millions of years ago when the great reptiles launched themselves from cliff tops above stormy oceans.

AAAAK! AAAAK!

He cried out in triumph and then had an urge to soar upwards, to fly higher and

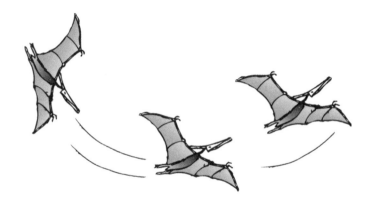

faster.

But he didn't. He flicked his wings round and wheeled away along the track, overtaking the train. Far below, his friends cheered him on. All except Steg who was watching grim faced.

In Dacky's beak was one of Steg's beautiful red tail lights.

Steg could see it winking in the sky like a strange star, getting smaller and smaller.

Protos' plan was simple. Dacky would fly ahead and leave the light by the side of the track. The train driver would think it was a signal to stop.

"Everybody, get ready to jump!" Protos called out above the roar of the wind.

Marlin came to stand next to him.

He looked at the ground rushing past.

"I hope Dacky can do it," he said.

Soon Dacky had got far enough ahead. He swooped low and spotted a good place. A tree with branches hanging close to the line. It was perfect, exactly the right height for a railway signal.

He landed smoothly and tucked Steg's light between two branches, then flapped off to hide in the undergrowth.

He had just got out of sight when the train came racing into view.

But sure enough the driver spotted the light and slammed on the brakes.

SCREEEEECH!

In the darkness the Dinoteks jumped and clambered down – Protos landed heavily, but quickly followed the others into the trees.

They kept very still in the dark for what seemed like ages.

Nothing moved.

Then at last the train hissed, clunked and moved forwards again, faster and faster until it was gone.

Dacky flew down and they rushed over to him.

"Well done! Brilliant flying!"

But Dacky wasn't smiling.

He hopped over to Steg.

"I'm sorry," he said. "I couldn't save your light. The train driver took it."

Steg sighed.

"It doesn't matter," he said. "At least we're all safe."

****

They walked away from the railway line. Steg went in front and lit up his armour to show them the way.

But now his tail only had three lights, not four.

"We'll get you another one," promised Protos. "It will be the best we can find."

"And I'll fit it for you," said Marlin.

"It's OK. I'm not worried," shrugged Steg. He was trying to sound cheerful.

They walked on, looking for somewhere to rest, and Protos told them all a story.

He talked about where they would be going. There were fossils in the ground there, layers and layers of them waiting to be discovered, some from creatures quite unknown. And he talked about all the things living in the woods – birds, mammals, insects, plants – and all the secret places there were to explore.

And then he stopped.

"Now it's time to sleep," he said.

The huddled together under a wide tree. The Troodons sheltered next to Steg. Dacky flapped up into one of the branches. Marlin curled up on the ground beside Flame and felt the warmth of his motor as it purred deep inside. And Protos settled down at the edge of the circle, looking out into the night.

****

Snickenbacker and Grubbler were having dinner when, at exactly midnight, the phone rang. It was Smith.

"No! That's impossible!"

For once Snickenbacker was not calm.

He screwed up his fist and thumped the dinner table so hard that the plates rattled.

"What is it? What's wrong?" exclaimed Grubbler.

"They escaped – again!" hissed Snickenbacker. "But how?!"

He stood up and began pacing around the room.

"It's impossible. They were on that

train…"

Then he walked across to his desk and sat down.

Grubbler watched him.

All at once, Snickenbacker's face didn't look angry any more – he smiled coldly and picked up his phone again.

"Smith? It's time. First thing tomorrow morning – wake up the *Raptor*…"

Chapter Fourteen

·················

Little Dragon

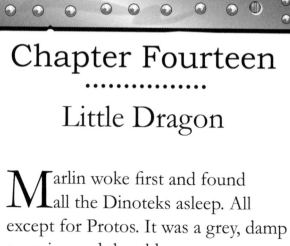

Marlin woke first and found all the Dinoteks asleep. All except for Protos. It was a grey, damp morning and the old creature was staring into the distance. There were trees all around them and far away hills with their tops hidden in mist.

"Hello Marlin! Did you get some rest?"

"Yes," Marlin yawned. "Did you?"

Protos shook his head.

"No! This time I stayed awake all night. I've spent too many years sleeping. Did you know the stars move across the sky?"

Marlin shook his head.

"They do if you watch them for long enough," said Protos. "They go circling overhead."

"And where are *we* going?" said a voice. It was Steg, now awake too.

"Somewhere safe," said Protos – but he wouldn't say any more about it, not until everyone was awake.

Marlin rummaged in his rucksack and grinned. Uncle Gus had packed breakfast for him too. It was almost as if he'd known that Marlin would be travelling!

He unwrapped the paper and found a chunky cheese sandwich inside. And there was a bottle of water.

I wonder what he's doing now? I hope he's not worried...

"Do you have a phone?" asked Protos suddenly, as if he'd guessed Marlin's thoughts.

Marlin shook his head.

"Hmm…" nodded the old creature, almost talking to himself. "We must find a phone…"

Then Protos bowed his head and seemed to close his eyes. One by one the Dinoteks woke up. Comp and Siggy began

scampering around
between the trees.
Dacky hopped down
from his branch and
Flame stretched and
yawned.

Protos didn't move.
Marlin watched him.
He seemed to be
waiting for something.

Finally, the sun came out and the old
creature looked up. He heaved himself
round to face them all.

"We can go now!" he said. "We've got a
long way to walk today but I'm sure you'll
all like it where we're going."

"But where *are* we going?" asked Marlin.

Protos looked at Flame.

"Do you have it? The thing I gave you?"

"Yes."

Flame turned his head and lifted the
bundle from his back. He laid it carefully on
the ground.

"There is a place called the Jurassic
Mountain," said Protos. "And we'll be safe
there."

"What about the bad people?" squeaked Comp.

"They won't be able to hurt us," said Protos. "Because of this…"

Protos unwrapped the bundle and pulled out a sheet of paper.

"This is very precious. The Professor left it for us."

"What is it?" cawed Dacky.

"It's called a Legal Document."

The Dinoteks gathered round and looked at it.

"It's just paper," frowned Steg. "With funny lines…"

"Words. Writing. It says the mountain belongs to us."

"A whole mountain?" exclaimed Marlin.

"Yes."

Protos picked up the paper and carefully handed it to Marlin.

"Will you look after this for us?"

Marlin nodded, and he opened his rucksack. There was a pocket inside and he slipped the paper into it.

"So where is it then?" asked Steg. "Where *is* the mountain?"

Protos shook his head.

"I don't know the way from here…"

Steg snorted.

"But there is someone who can help us," continued Protos.

He reached down and pulled at the cloth again. Something rolled out and everyone gasped.

****

There, lying on the ground, was an enormous dragonfly. It had a long, thin body – only just smaller than the Troodons – and four slender wings, neatly folded.

"Another Dinotek!" cheered Marlin.

"Yes," smiled Protos.

"He's cute!" squeaked Siggy. "So tiny!"

"Can he fly?" cawed Dacky.

"Yes," said Protos. "He's a Meganeura and his name is Little Dragon."

Marlin delved into his rucksack again.

"I can charge his battery!"

"No need," said Protos. "Look. He's powered by the sun!"

And sure enough, as they watched the

little creature began to move. Its wings
flickered and twitched and then they
spread open.

It lay still for a moment longer, taking in
the heat, then suddenly its wings buzzed
and it flew up into the air.

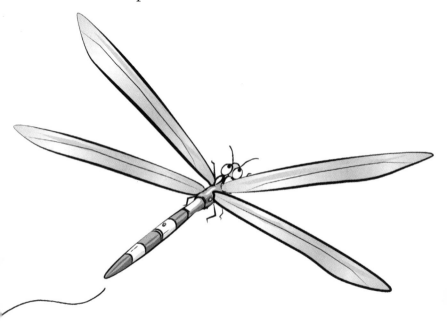

"Hello Little Dragon," laughed Protos.
"Do you know where we are?"

The creature buzzed around, flitting
away through the trees, then it came back
and perched on Protos' horn.

"We're lost! Can you show us the way to

the mountain?"

The Meganeura took off again and flew away.

"Quickly now," said Protos. "Follow after him everyone!"

They all set off, striding, running, clunking and scampering – chasing through the trees – and it was such fun that even Steg couldn't help laughing.

The only one who didn't run was Dacky.

He wouldn't stay on the ground now! He spread his great wings and took to the air.

****

And at that very moment, far away in the south, the *Raptor* was taking to the air too.

It was Howard Snickenbacker's favourite machine – his hunting helicopter.

Its sharp rotor-blades spun faster and faster, chopping at the air. Then it left the ground.

It picked up speed. It soared over the city and headed north, following the railway line.

End of Part Two

– – –

Can't wait
to finish the story?

Read the start of
Book 3 now...

The Secret Dinosaur

Jurassic Adventure

The Dinotek Adventures
—— Book 3 ——
It's the moment of truth...

Chapter One

Plunging In

Marlin Maxton was just an ordinary boy until he reached the age of ten. And then, when he was exactly ten years and two months old, he became the luckiest boy ever.

Can you imagine having a full-size T-Rex for a friend? And escaping with a family of dinosaurs on a train in the middle of the night? And going to live with them on a mountain?

Well Marlin Maxton was even luckier than that.

Marlin's friends were *Dinoteks*. Living dinosaur machines – which meant they could think and talk and fly and run incredibly fast. And they also had all sorts of amazing powers.

Which was lucky, because right now

Marlin really needed help…

****

He was clutching onto the root of a tree as he dangled over the edge of a steep bank with his feet in a river. The cold water was filling his trainers, soaking up his trouser legs. He looked down again and felt a lurch of fear. The river was flowing fast and deep.

"Help!" he shouted. "Flame! Quick!"

There was no reply.

Marlin was carrying a heavy rucksack and that made it hard for him to move and hard to hang on. His fingers slipped on the muddy tree root.

He thought fast (as people do when they find themselves in immediate danger).

One: the bag was heavy. If he was still wearing it when he fell into water he would sink like a stone.

Two: he couldn't just drop the bag because inside it were many precious things that he'd spent a long time collecting. And, even more importantly, in the bag was also the one thing that the Dinoteks needed to survive: the golden power-charger that restored their batteries and gave them energy. If that went into the river it might never work again.

And three…

But before he got to three his fingers slipped again and he heard himself crying out.

"Help!"

****

Marlin had spent a whole week living on the mountain, being very adventurous and resourceful. He'd even begun to think of himself as someone quite brave. But now his voice sounded different. It came out like a frightened squeak.

"I'm falling!"

And then, just in time, he saw it…

A broken root sticking out of the bank just below him.

Use it as a hook! Hang the bag there…

With the last of his strength Marlin managed to get the precious bag onto the

sticking-out-root.

And a second later he fell.

Marlin fell and just before the cold water engulfed him another thought raced through his mind. Why had he called Flame anyway? The Dinotek T-Rex couldn't help him.

Continued in Book 3...

About the author

N.S.Blackman has been writing and illustrating dinosaur stories since his early school days
in the Cretaceous era.

After emerging onto dry land he worked as a cleaner, a shop assistant, a teacher and a journalist before eventually evolving into his present form as a writer and illustrator.
His current habitat is London where he lives not far from Crystal Palace (where the world's oldest life-size dinosaur models also have their home).

If you have any questions about the Dinoteks or would like to send in your own designs and pictures to N.S.Blackman you can find him on Facebook or at www.dinoteks.com